For Sheryl, world traveller, with love. — TM

For Cody and Raven, forever faithful and always by my side. — TS

A Canadian YEAR

TWELVE MONTHS IN THE LIFE OF CANADA'S KIDS

TANIA MCCARTNEY + TINA SNERLING

Welcome to Canada

Salut! Je m'appelle *CHLOE* et j'ai 7 ans. We speak both French and English at home. I love art, music and dance, and when I'm older, I want to be a singer.

Ai, I'm OKI. I'm 8 years old and my family are Inuit. We speak Inuktitut. I love travel, languages and science, and I'd love to become a pediatrician one day.

Ni hao! My name is AVA and I'm 9. My mom is from China and my dad is from Québec. I love soccer and cooking, and when I grow up, I want to be a chef.

Hey, I'm LIAM. My family came to Canada from Scotland. I'm 10, and I love snowboarding and computer games. One day, I want to be a computer programmer.

Hi! My name is NOAH and I'm 6 years old. I love reading, football and hiking in the mountains. When I'm big, I want to play hockey for the Vancouver Canucks!

January

It's -30°C but we still go **SKIING**, skating and tobogganing.

BONNE ANNÉE!

1

It's NEW YEAR'S DAY!

WOOF!

Sled races are AWESOME!

There's a lot to keep us **BUSY** after school.

HOMEWORK

HOCKEY PRACTICE

VIDEO GAMES

6

QUI EST LE ROI?

La FÊTE des Rois.

DOUGHNUTS AND DOUGHNUT HOLES

COOKIES

CHIPS

CHEESE AND CRACKERS

FRUIT

We have lots of favourite **SNACKS**.

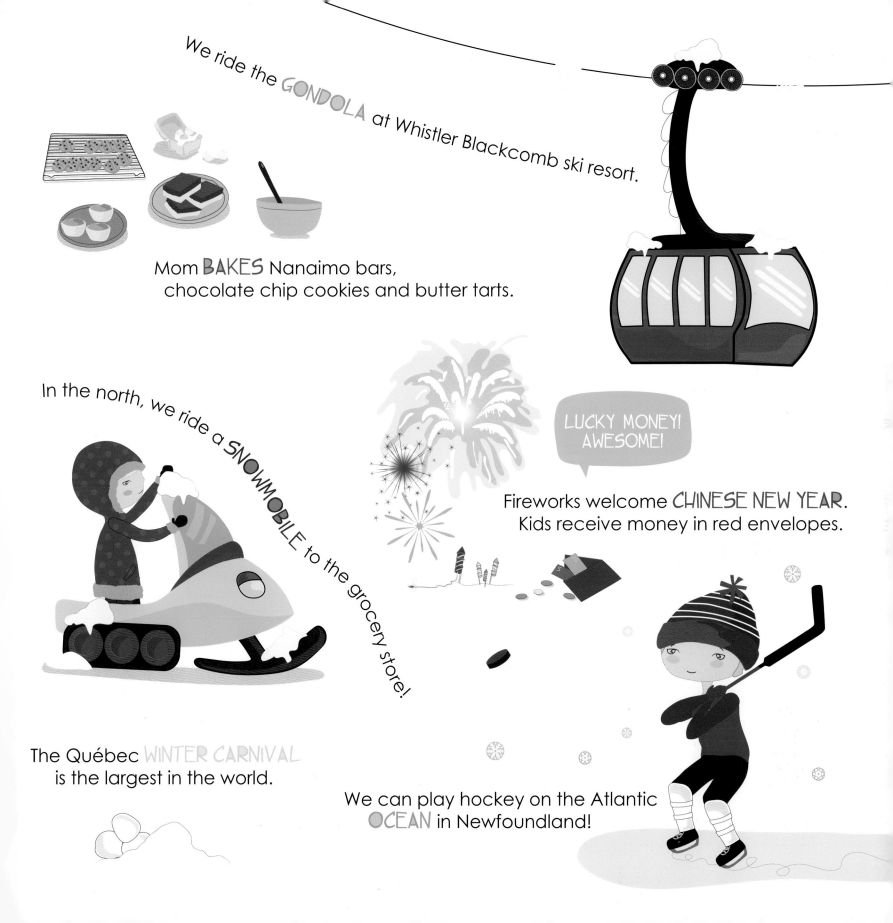

We ride the GONDOLA at Whistler Blackcomb ski resort.

Mom BAKES Nanaimo bars, chocolate chip cookies and butter tarts.

In the north, we ride a SNOWMOBILE to the grocery store!

LUCKY MONEY! AWESOME!

Fireworks welcome CHINESE NEW YEAR. Kids receive money in red envelopes.

The Québec WINTER CARNIVAL is the largest in the world.

We can play hockey on the Atlantic OCEAN in Newfoundland!

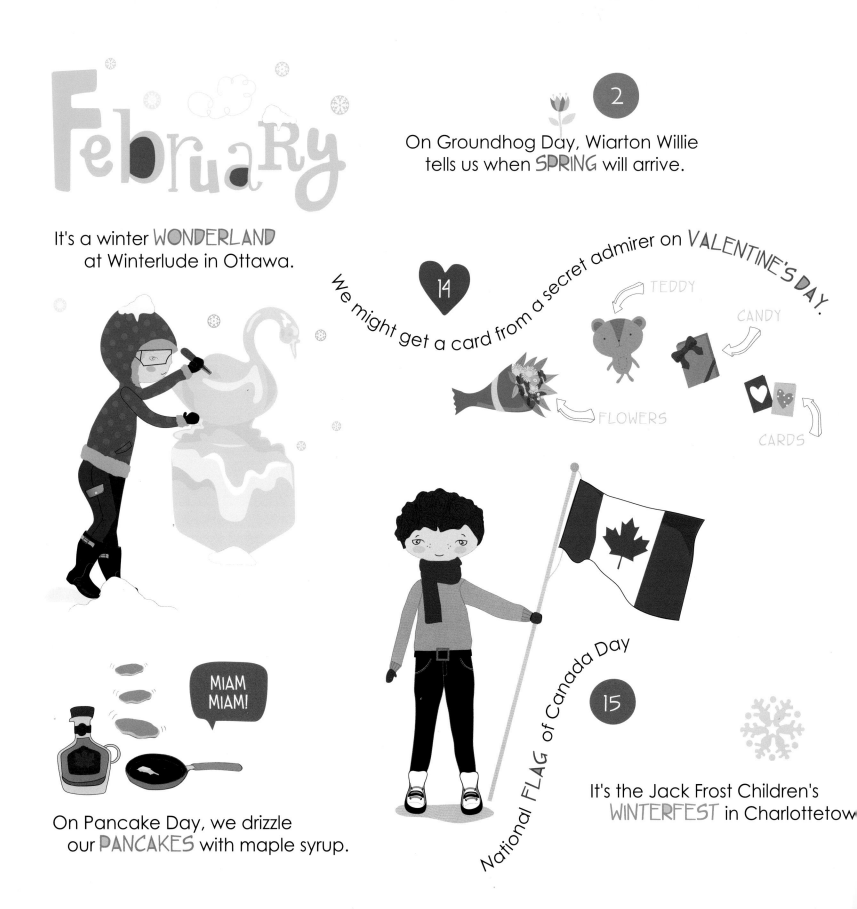

February

It's a winter WONDERLAND at Winterlude in Ottawa.

On Pancake Day, we drizzle our PANCAKES with maple syrup.

MIAM MIAM!

2 On Groundhog Day, Wiarton Willie tells us when SPRING will arrive.

14 we might get a card from a secret admirer on VALENTINE'S DAY.

TEDDY
CANDY
FLOWERS
CARDS

National FLAG of Canada Day

15 It's the Jack Frost Children's WINTERFEST in Charlottetow

March

March means SPRING!

Beavers, raccoons and caribou wander the FOREST near our house.

Québec's Hôtel de Glace is made of ICE and SNOW!

SCIENCE IS COOL!

EPIC!

GREEN BEAR

HORNS

SHAMROCKS

GREEN HATS

17

The world's largest SKATING RINK, Rideau Canal in Ottawa, starts to thaw.

We visit TELUS World of SCIENCE in Edmonton.

Montréal's ST PATRICK'S DAY parade is epic!

The skies over our PRAIRIES are so very high.

On GOOD Friday, we nibble hot cross buns, all melty with butter.

It's spring BREAK! Time for Easter, which sometimes falls in April.

CHOCOLATE EGGS

DAFFODILS

CHICKS

QUICK! GET IN THE CAR!

BUNNIES

CANADA : 17

On Easter Sunday, we decorate eggs and go on an EGG HUNT. We eat mustard-crusted lamb and Easter basket cake.

DAYLIGHT SAVING begins. Clocks go forward.

Polar BEARS wander the streets of Churchill, Manitoba.

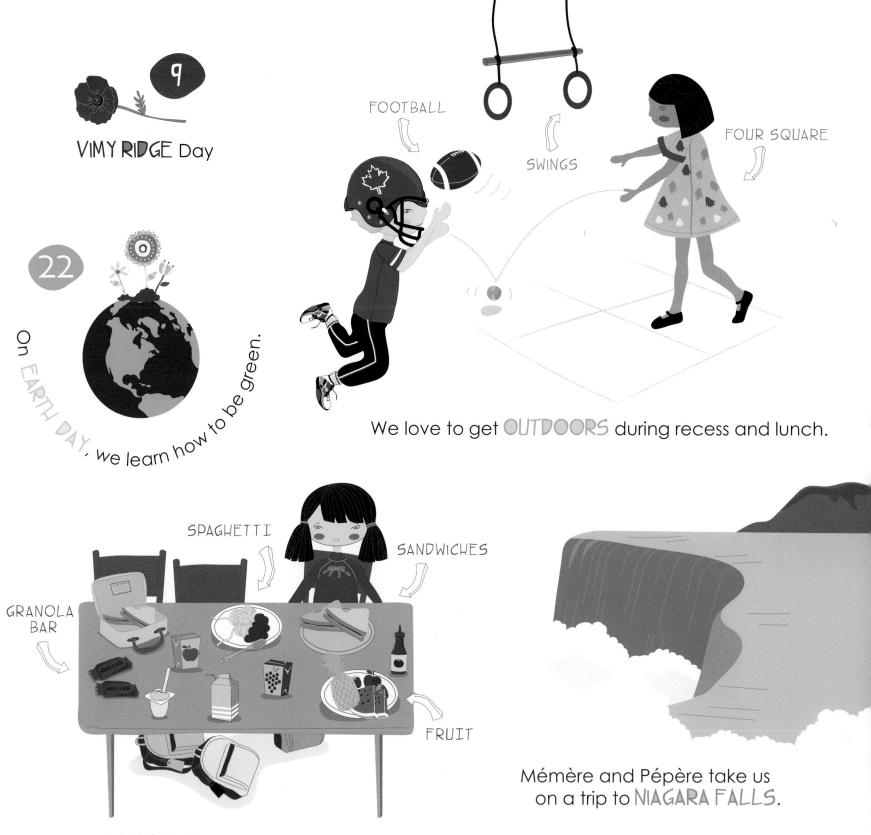

9

VIMY RIDGE Day

22

On EARTH DAY, we learn how to be green.

FOOTBALL

SWINGS

FOUR SQUARE

We love to get OUTDOORS during recess and lunch.

GRANOLA BAR

SPAGHETTI

SANDWICHES

FRUIT

We take a LUNCHBOX to school, or eat in the cafeteria.

Mémère and Pépère take us on a trip to NIAGARA FALLS.

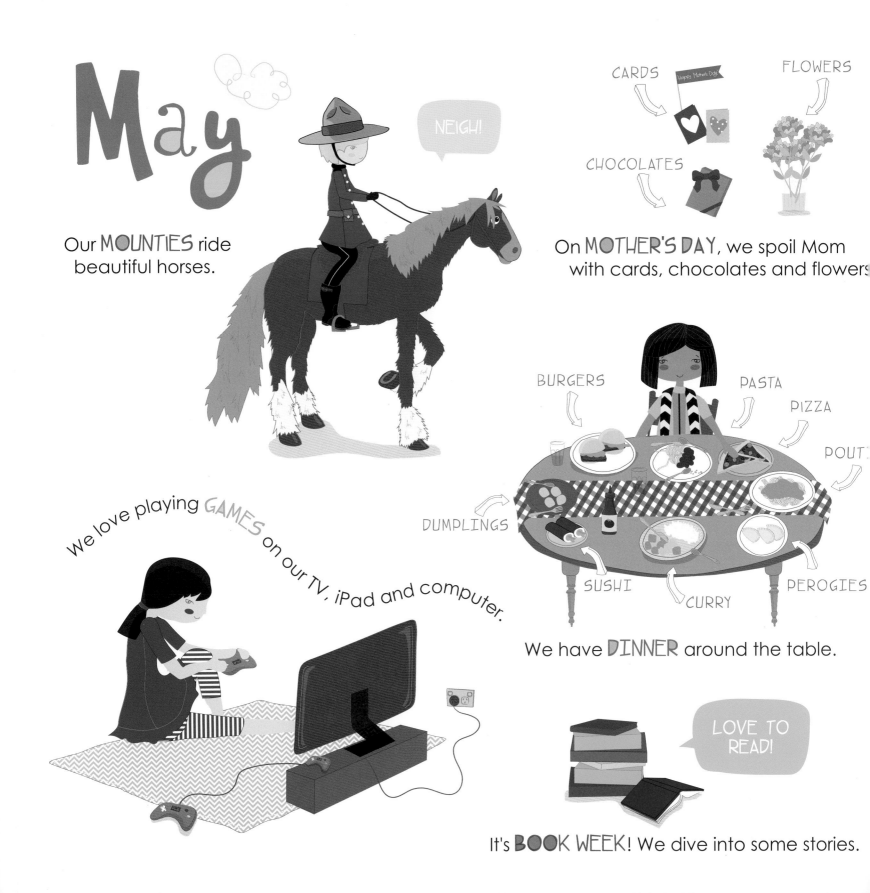

May

Our MOUNTIES ride beautiful horses.

NEIGH!

On MOTHER'S DAY, we spoil Mom with cards, chocolates and flowers.

CARDS

FLOWERS

CHOCOLATES

We love playing GAMES on our TV, iPad and computer.

BURGERS

PASTA

PIZZA

POUT

DUMPLINGS

SUSHI

CURRY

PEROGIES

We have DINNER around the table.

LOVE TO READ!

It's BOOK WEEK! We dive into some stories.

There are a million BLOOMS at the Canadian Tulip Festival!

PRETTY!

VICTORIA Day

It's WARMING up. We ride our bikes, go skateboarding or play soccer in the park.

We celebrate our CULTURE with powwows and potlatches.

GUMMIES

CHERRY LICORICE

MINTS

CHOCOLATE

We like CANDY!

JELLYSTONE PARK

Yogi Bear lives at JELLYSTONE Park.

It's the Ottawa CHILDREN'S Festival.

We have sleepovers and playdates with FRIENDS.

June

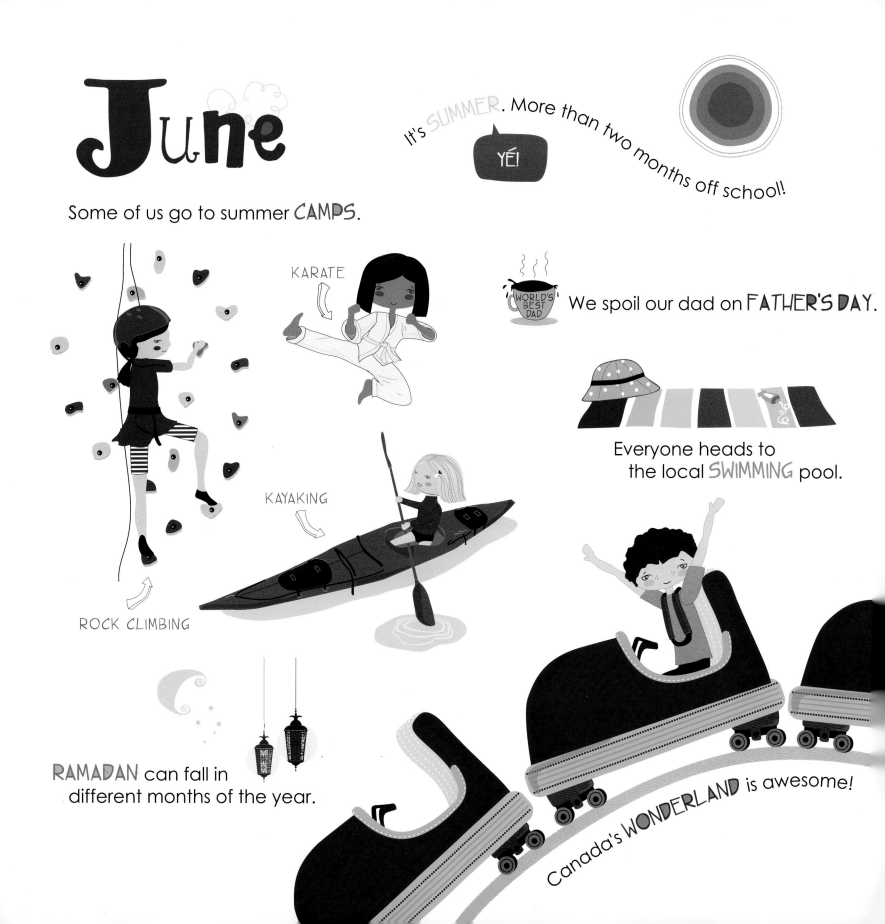

It's SUMMER. More than two months off school!!

YÉ!

Some of us go to summer CAMPS.

KARATE

We spoil our dad on FATHER'S DAY.

WORLD'S BEST DAD

Everyone heads to the local SWIMMING pool.

ROCK CLIMBING

KAYAKING

RAMADAN can fall in different months of the year.

Canada's WONDERLAND is awesome!

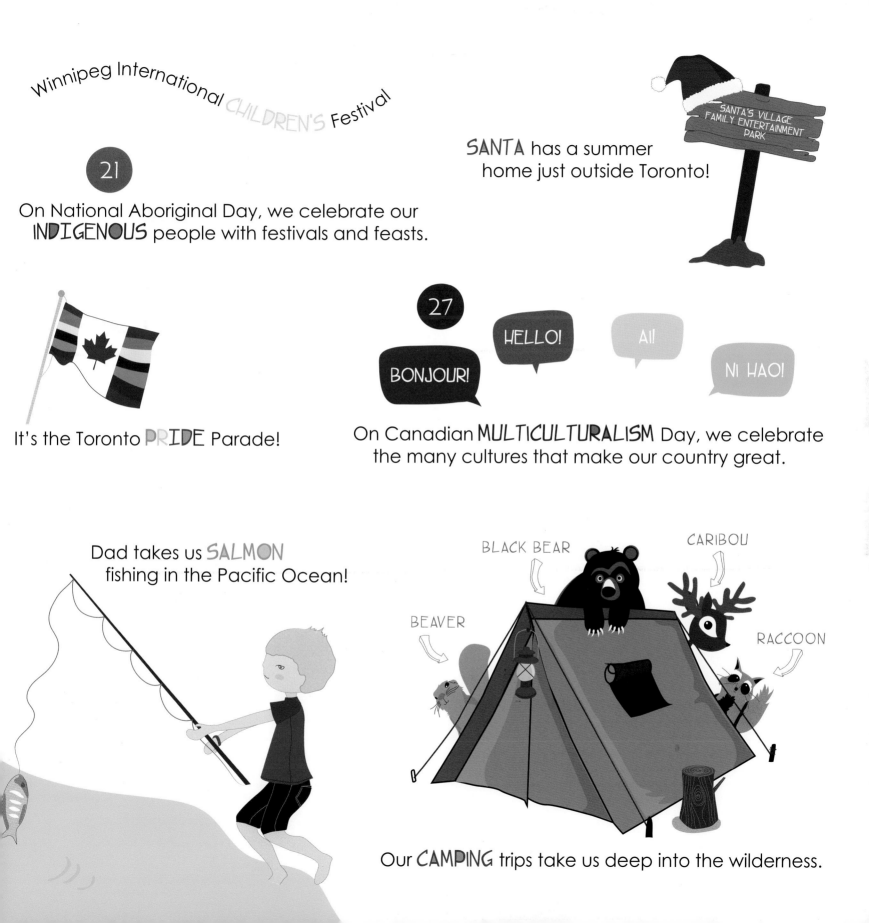

Winnipeg International CHILDREN'S Festival

21

On National Aboriginal Day, we celebrate our **INDIGENOUS** people with festivals and feasts.

SANTA'S VILLAGE FAMILY ENTERTAINMENT PARK

SANTA has a summer home just outside Toronto!

It's the Toronto **PRIDE** Parade!

27

BONJOUR!

HELLO!

AI!

NI HAO!

On Canadian **MULTICULTURALISM** Day, we celebrate the many cultures that make our country great.

Dad takes us **SALMON** fishing in the Pacific Ocean!

BLACK BEAR

CARIBOU

BEAVER

RACCOON

Our **CAMPING** trips take us deep into the wilderness.

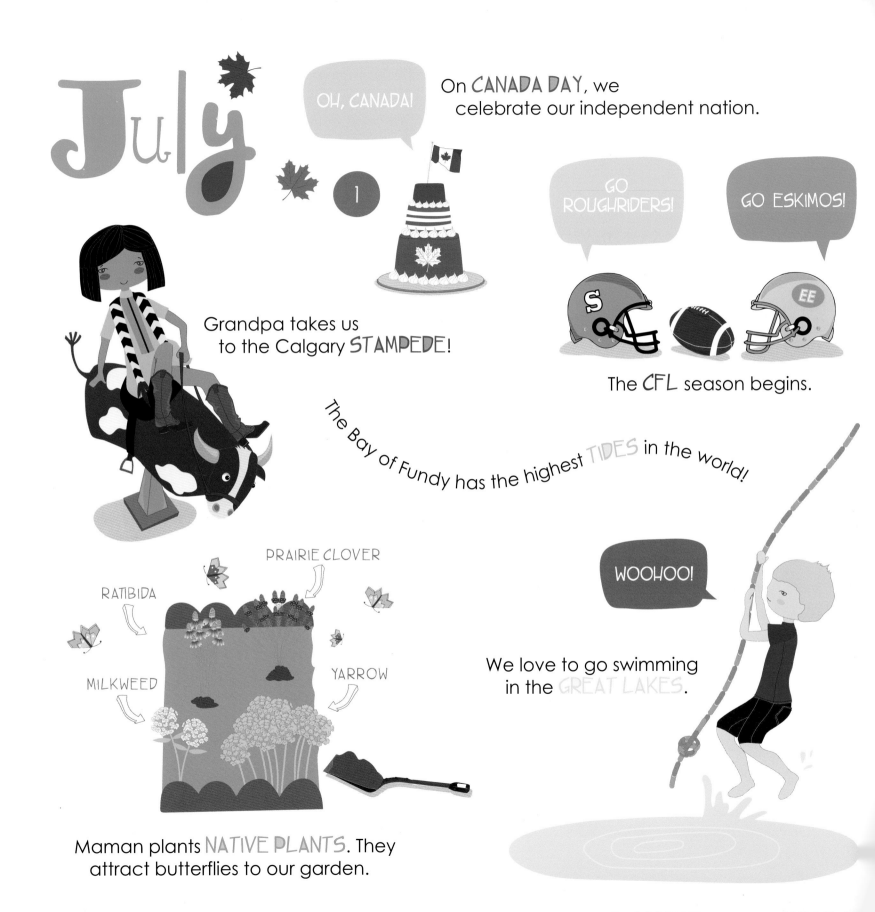

Celebration of Light in Vancouver is a spectacular musical FIREWORKS competition.

WOW!

ORCAS can be spotted off the coast of Vancouver.

LEMONADE JUICE MILK WATER

We COOL down with our favourite drinks.

Our family has a weiner roast on the BEACH.

Granville Island Water Park is SPLASHING good fun.

August

Piikani Nation Annual Celebration is Canada's oldest POWWOW event.

August LONG WEEKEND

SEAL
WHALE
DULSE CHIPS
BEAVERTAILS
POUTINE
FIGGY DUFF

We have some pretty QUIRKY Canadian foods.

FREEZIES cool us down.

National PEACEKEEPERS' Day

AH, THE GREAT OUTDOORS!

Our allowance is paid in LOONIES and TOONIES.

Papa takes us camping on LAKE SUPERIOR. We hunt, fish and swim.

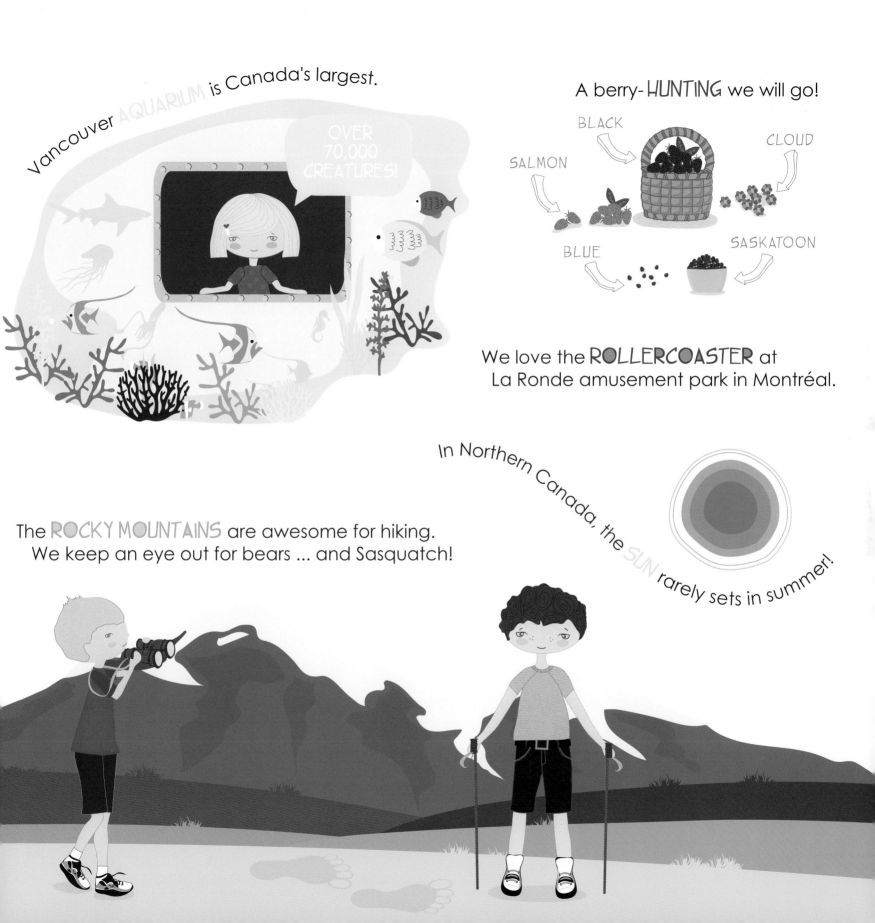

Vancouver AQUARIUM is Canada's largest.

OVER 70,000 CREATURES!

A berry-HUNTING we will go!

BLACK

SALMON

CLOUD

BLUE

SASKATOON

We love the ROLLERCOASTER at
La Ronde amusement park in Montréal.

In Northern Canada, the SUN rarely sets in summer!

The ROCKY MOUNTAINS are awesome for hiking.
We keep an eye out for bears ... and Sasquatch!

September

ALSO CALLED AUTUMN

It's FALL. Leaves start to turn.

The SCHOOL YEAR begins.

On LABOUR DAY, we go to a local fair, have a picnic or watch football on TV.

FÊTE DU TRAVAIL

BANNOCK   WAFFLES

EGGS

HONEY

MILK

CEREAL   SMOOTHIE   PANCAKES

BREAKFAST is scrumptious at our house.

We tell tales at the Telling Tales children's LITERARY FESTIVAL in Rockton, Ontario.

Local MOOSE, bears and raccoons knock over our garbage can!

We go on a field trip to the MARITIME Museum of the Atlantic in Halifax.

National GRANDPARENTS' Day

LEGO

BOARD GAMES

DOLLS

CABLE SHIPS

On RAINY days, we play inside.

The Canadian Aboriginal Festival celebrates our FIRST NATIONS people.

OOOH!

PUMPKIN

APPLES

CORN

MAPLE SYRUP

The NORTHERN LIGHTS are a sight to behold.

Local FESTIVALS are held around Canada all through the year.

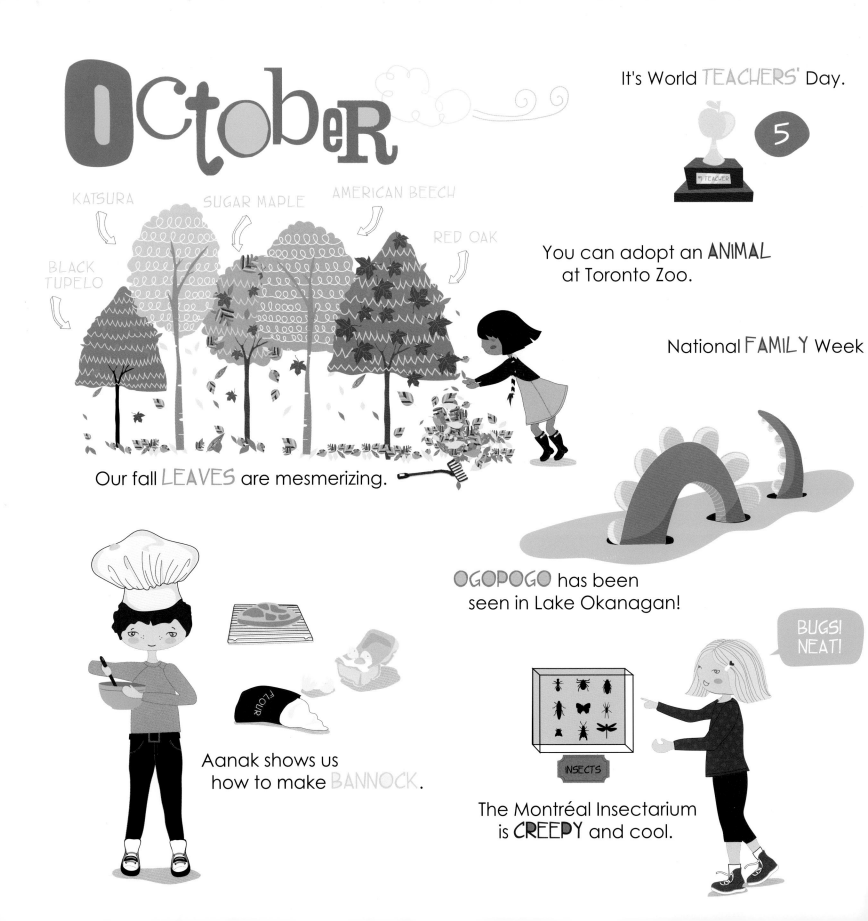

OCTOBER

It's World TEACHERS' Day.

5

KATSURA
SUGAR MAPLE
AMERICAN BEECH
RED OAK
BLACK TUPELO

You can adopt an ANIMAL at Toronto Zoo.

National FAMILY Week

Our fall LEAVES are mesmerizing.

OGOPOGO has been seen in Lake Okanagan!

FLOUR

BUGS! NEAT!

Aanak shows us how to make BANNOCK.

INSECTS

The Montréal Insectarium is CREEPY and cool.

On THANKSGIVING, we feast with family and friends. Some of us go hiking or fishing.

SECOND MONDAY IN OCTOBER

Migrating BIRDS fly high in the skies above.

WHOOPING CRANE

GOLDEN EAGLE

CANADA GOOSE

TUNDRA GOOSE

There are farm animals, corn mazes and hayrides at our local PUMPKIN PATCH.

Dad loves OKTOBERFEST!

BOO!

R.I.P.

31

It's HALLOWEEN! We trick-or-treat, carve pumpkins, and gobble toffee apples and candy.

November

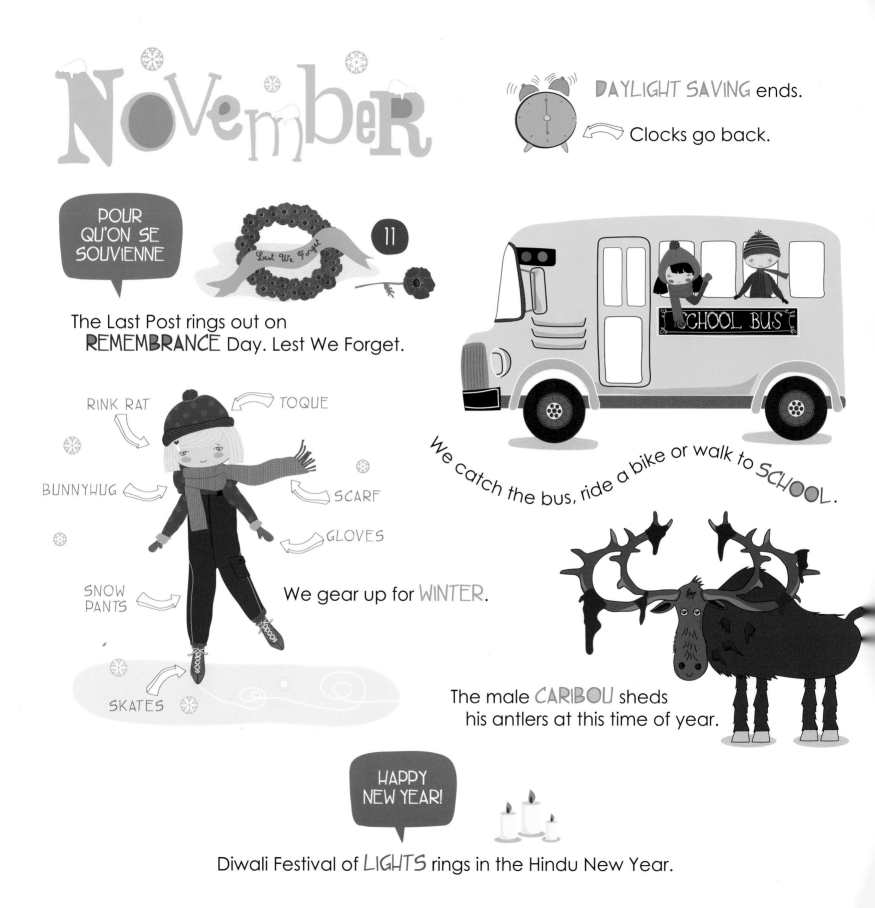

DAYLIGHT SAVING ends.

Clocks go back.

POUR QU'ON SE SOUVIENNE

11

Lest We Forget

The Last Post rings out on REMEMBRANCE Day. Lest We Forget.

SCHOOL BUS

We catch the bus, ride a bike or walk to SCHOOL.

RINK RAT

TOQUE

BUNNYHUG

SCARF

GLOVES

SNOW PANTS

We gear up for WINTER.

SKATES

The male CARIBOU sheds his antlers at this time of year.

HAPPY NEW YEAR!

Diwali Festival of LIGHTS rings in the Hindu New Year.

THIS WAY, PLEASE!

In Banff National Park, the WILDLIFE have overpasses!

Grandma shows us how to weave DREAM CATCHERS.

20

It's Universal CHILDREN'S Day.

The WINTER FESTIVAL of Lights in Niagara Falls begins.

In Northern Canada, our HOMES are built on stilts so the ground below doesn't melt!

SLANTED ROOF

SMALL WINDOWS

STILTS

PERMAFROST

'INUIT' means 'the people'. Our anoraks are made from caribou hide and sealskin.

December

WINTER is here. It's all snowball fights and snow forts.

Our Christmas tree smells like the FOREST.

LIGHTS

RIBBON

TINSEL

BAUBLES

xmas decorations

We make gingerbread and write in CHRISTMAS cards.

CALGARY ROUGHNECKS!

TORONTO ROCK!

The National LACROSSE League season begins.

10 It's HUMAN RIGHTS DAY.

The Santa Claus parade in Toronto is MASSIVE!

HANUKKAH

We eat maple syrup TAFFY, barley candy and chicken bones!

JE M'APPELLE PÈRE NOËL

French families enjoy RÉVEILLON on Christmas Eve.
We dine on tourtières and bûche de Noël.

On Christmas Eve, we track Santa's journey online.
Some of us open PRESENTS or go to Midnight Mass.

It's Christmas HOLIDAYS!

24

SINCK TUCK is celebrated
with dancing and gift-giving.

ROAST TURKEY

HAM

GRAVY

CRANBERRY SAUCE

PEAS

MASHED POTATO

PLUM PUDDING

APPLE PIE

25

On CHRISTMAS DAY, we open
presents and enjoy a delicious feast.

BONNE ANNÉE!

31

It's BOXING Day.   26

We go ice-fishing on NEW YEAR'S EVE.
Fireworks pop to welcome in a brand new year.

Our Country

THE PROVINCES AND TERRITORIES OF CANADA

Alberta
British Columbia
Manitoba
New Brunswick
Newfoundland and Labrador
Nova Scotia
Ontario
Prince Edward Island
Québec
Saskatchewan
Northwest Territories
Nunavut
Yukon

CANADA IS THE WORLD'S SECOND-LARGEST COUNTRY

THE NORTH AMERICAN BEAVER IS OUR NATIONAL ANIMAL

AFTER PARIS, MONTRÉAL IS THE LARGEST FRENCH-SPEAKING CITY IN THE WORLD

CANADA HAS THE LONGEST COASTLINE IN THE WORLD

Canada comes from the native word 'kanata' meaning village.

A huge thank you to Canadian advisors Kathy Bobyn, Helen Busetti, and to the kids of Ripple Rock Elementary, British Columbia. Thanks also to the following people for their contribution: Ellen Warwick, Iolanda Millar, Jacques Filippi, Jean Cichon, Kristina Koski, Peter Hill-Field, Tim Gain and Tracey Bhangu. Unending thanks to Anouska Jones and the team at Exisle for their support. — TM + TS

First published 2017

EK Books
an imprint of Exisle Publishing Pty Ltd
P.O. Box 864, Chatswood, NSW 2057, Australia
P.O. Box 60490, Titirangi, Auckland, 0642, New Zealand
www.ekbooks.org

Copyright © 2017 in text: Tania McCartney
Copyright © 2017 in illustrations: Tina Snerling
Tania McCartney and Tina Snerling assert the moral right to be identified as the creators of this work.

All rights reserved. Except for short extracts for the purpose of review, no part of this book may be reproduced, stored in a retrieval system or transmitted in any form or by any means, whether electronic, mechanical, photocopying, recording or otherwise, without prior written permission from the publisher.

A CiP record for this book is available from the National Library of Australia

ISBN 978 1 925335 43 9

Designed and typeset by Tina Snerling
Typeset in Century Gothic, Street Cred and custom fonts
Printed in China
This book uses paper sourced under ISO 1 4001 guidelines from well-managed forests and other controlled sources.

10 9 8 7 6 5 4 3 2

Author Note

This is by no means a comprehensive listing of the events and traditions celebrated by Canada's multitude of ethnic people. The entries in this book have been chosen to reflect a range of modern lifestyles for the majority of Canada's children, with a focus on traditional endemic elements and themes, which are in themselves a glorious mishmash of present, past, introduced and endemic culture. Content in this book has been produced in consultation with native Canadian advisors, school teachers, and school children, with every intention of respecting the cultural and idiosyncratic elements of Canada and its people.